Alfred's
Book of Monsters

Sam Streed

Alfred's
Book of Monsters

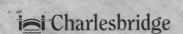

Charlesbridge

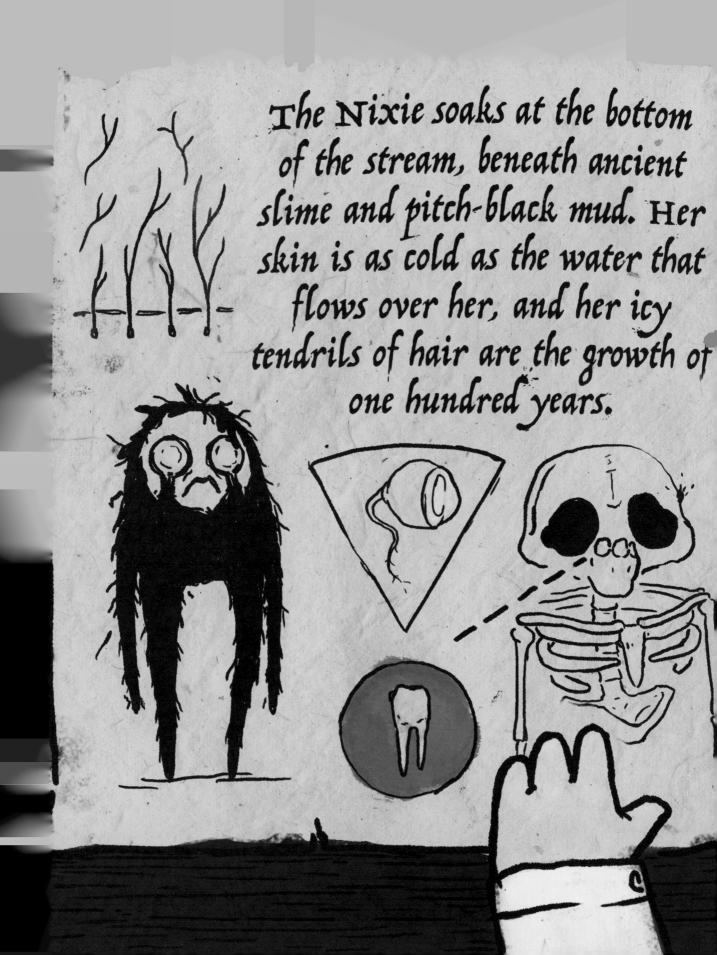

The Nixie soaks at the bottom of the stream, beneath ancient slime and pitch-black mud. Her skin is as cold as the water that flows over her, and her icy tendrils of hair are the growth of one hundred years.

"Whoa . . ."

"Alfred, quit reading that
dreadful book! It is tea time!"

Alfred hated teatime.

"It's perfectly delightful," he said.
Alfred didn't enjoy delightful things.

Still, he went to have tea
with his aunty.

The next day, Alfred was once again locked away in his study.

He read more about the monsters
that lurked in the shadows of his
little town.

In the graveyard, between stone monuments to forgotten souls, lurks the Black Shuck. Its footfall make no sound. Its cry cuts through the silence of the night. Its one blood-red eye burns with an undying rage.

"Whoa . . ."

"Alfred! Teatime!"

It was delightful, as always.

Alfred complained to Aunty that
he didn't want delightful things.

He wanted **terrible** things.
"I want MONSTERS!"

To Alfred's dismay, Aunty
didn't approve.

"Monsters are terrible," she said.

"Polite young boys do
not hate tea parties, and they
certainly do not want monsters!"

The next day . . .

Alfred was back to reading
his favorite book.

In the darkest and most secret corners and closets of the church lives the Lantern Man, a spirit whose light shreds the dark of the night. The flame he carries is the light of one thousand stolen souls.

"Whoa. . . . That's it!
I must see them for myself."

So Alfred got to work.

For once, Alfred was excited
for teatime.

At last, from the darkening night
came three fearsome knocks.

And they all had a **terrible** time.

For Jack, who can't read yet.

Published by Charlesbridge, 85 Main Street,
Watertown, MA 02472 • (617) 926-0329
www.charlesbridge.com

Printed in China
(hc) 10 9 8 7 6 5 4 3 2 1

Illustrations done in Photoshop by scanning and combining
old paper, ink splotches, and spooky sketches influenced
by antique books and an old-fashioned Victorian world.
Display type set in P22 Mayflower and Goudy
Text type set in P22 Stickley
Printed by 1010 Printing International Limited
in Huizhou, Guangdong, China
Production supervision by Brian G. Walker
Designed by Susan Mallory Sherman

Library of Congress Cataloging-in-
Publication Data

Names: Streed, Sam, author, illustrator.
Title: Alfred's book of monsters / Sam Streed.
Description: Watertown, MA : Charlesbridge,
[2019] | Summary: Alfred loves the monsters in
his book, but he doesn't like teatime with his
aunt—until he decides to invite three of his
favorite monsters to join him for tea.
Identifiers: LCCN 2018026282 (print) | LCCN
2018031934 (ebook) | ISBN 9781632897190
(ebook) | ISBN 9781632897206 (ebook pdf) |
ISBN 9781580898331 (reinforced for library use)
Subjects: LCSH: Monsters—Juvenile fiction.
| Aunts—Juvenile fiction. | Afternoon
teas—Juvenile fiction. | Humorous stories. |
CYAC: Monsters—Fiction. | Aunts—Fiction. |
Afternoon teas—Fiction. | Humorous stories. |
LCGFT: Humorous fiction.
Classification: LCC PZ7.1.S793 (ebook) | LCC
PZ7.1.S793 Al 2019 (print) |DDC [E]—dc23
LC record available at
https://lccn.loc.gov/2018026282